A Note to Parents and Caregivers:

Read-it! Readers are for children who are just starting on the amazing road to reading. These beautiful books support both the acquisition of reading skills and the love of books.

The RED LEVEL presents familiar topics using common words and repeating sentence patterns.
The BLUE LEVEL presents new ideas using a larger vocabulary and varied sentence structure.
The YELLOW LEVEL presents more challenging ideas, a broad vocabulary, and wide variety in sentence structure.

When sharing a book with your child, read in short stretches, pausing often to talk about the pictures. Have your child turn the pages and point to the pictures and familiar words. And be sure to reread favorite stories or parts of stories.

There is no right or wrong way to share books with children. Find time to read with your child and pass on the legacy of literacy.

Adria F. Klein, Ph.D.
Professor Emeritus
California State University
San Bernardino, California

First American edition published in 2003 by
Picture Window Books
5115 Excelsior Boulevard
Suite 232
Minneapolis, MN 55416
1-877-845-8392
www.picturewindowbooks.com

First published in Great Britain by Franklin Watts, 96 Leonard Street, London, EC2A 4XD
Text © Penny Dolan 2000
Illustration © Leo Broadley 2000

Printed in the United States of America.
1 2 3 4 5 6 08 07 06 05 04 03

Library of Congress Cataloging-in-Publication
Dolan, Penny.
  Eight enormous elephants / written by Penny Dolan ; illustrated by Leo Broadley.—1st
American ed.
    p. cm. — (Read-it! readers)
  Summary: A boy asks to keep the mouse who made eight enormous elephants clean up
after themselves after they rampaged through the house.
  ISBN 1-4048-0054-9
  [1. Elephants—Fiction. 2. Mice—Fiction. 3. Stories in rhyme.] I. Broadley, Leo, ill. II. Title.
III. Series.
  PZ8.3.D68 Ei 2003
  [E]—dc21   2002074925

PiCTURE WiNDOW BOOKS

Read-it! Readers
Yellow Level

Eight Enormous Elephants

Written by Penny Dolan

Illustrated by Leo Broadley

Reading Advisors:
Adria F. Klein, Ph.D.
Professor Emeritus, California State University
San Bernardino, California

Ruth Thomas
Durham Public Schools
Durham, North Carolina

R. Ernice Bookout
Durham Public Schools
Durham, North Carolina

Picture Window Books
Minneapolis, Minnesota

Not just now, but a little
bit before,

eight enormous elephants
came in through the door.

They smashed the sofa, and
they jumped on the chairs.

They danced on the table,

and they slid down the stairs.

9

They splashed in the sink
and sploshed in the bath.

They bounced on the beds
and laughed and laughed.

They opened the cupboards
and looked in the drawers.

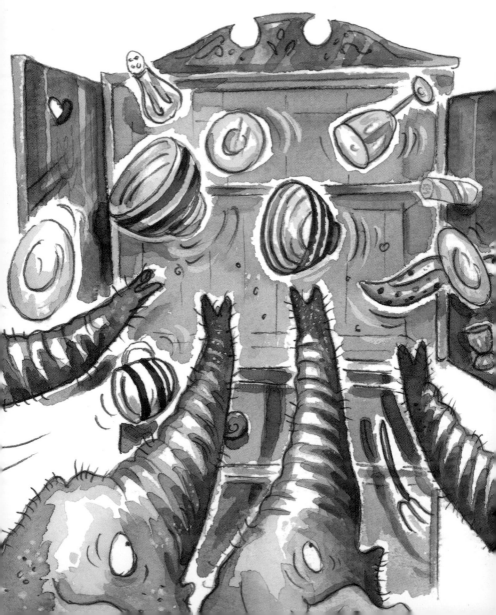

They slipped and skated
all over the floors.

I told them to go, but they said, "No way!" Then all of a sudden, a voice squeaked . . .

"You fix that sofa and straighten those chairs.

Go wipe that table and sweep those stairs.

Just rinse that sink and
the mess that's in it.

Go scrub that bath this very minute!

Make those beds, and
close those drawers.

Wash those prints off all
the floors!"

Then as soon as the house
was as clean as before . . .

the enormous elephants danced out of the door.

They danced away, and
they left no track.

But those enormous
elephants might come back!

So, what do you think, Mom?
What do you say?
Can I keep this mouse
that I found today?

eek!

PEPPER

Red Level

The Best Snowman, by Margaret Nash 1-4048-0048-4
Bill's Baggy Pants, by Susan Gates 1-4048-0050-6
Cleo and Leo, by Anne Cassidy 1-4048-0049-2
Felix on the Move, by Maeve Friel 1-4048-0055-7
Jasper and Jess, by Anne Cassidy 1-4048-0061-1
The Lazy Scarecrow, by Jillian Powell 1-4048-0062-X
Little Joe's Big Race, by Andy Blackford 1-4048-0063-8
The Little Star, by Deborah Nash 1-4048-0065-4
The Naughty Puppy, by Jillian Powell 1-4048-0067-0
Selfish Sophie, by Damian Kelleher 1-4048-0069-7

Blue Level

The Bossy Rooster, by Margaret Nash 1-4048-0051-4
Jack's Party, by Ann Bryant 1-4048-0060-3
Little Red Riding Hood, by Maggie Moore 1-4048-0064-6
Recycled!, by Jillian Powell 1-4048-0068-9
The Sassy Monkey, by Anne Cassidy 1-4048-0058-1
The Three Little Pigs, by Maggie Moore 1-4048-0071-9

Yellow Level

Cinderella, by Barrie Wade 1-4048-0052-2
The Crying Princess, by Anne Cassidy 1-4048-0053-0
Eight Enormous Elephants, by Penny Dolan 1-4048-0054-9
Freddie's Fears, by Hilary Robinson 1-4048-0056-5
Goldilocks and the Three Bears, by Barrie Wade 1-4048-0057-3
Mary and the Fairy, by Penny Dolan 1-4048-0066-2
Jack and the Beanstalk, by Maggie Moore 1-4048-0059-X
The Three Billy Goats Gruff, by Barrie Wade 1-4048-0070-0